Mystery at the Mall

Marian Hostetler

Illustrated by Gwen Stamm

HERALD PRESS
Scottdale, Pennsylvania
Kitchener, Ontario
1985

Library of Congress Cataloging-in-Publication Data

Hostetler, Marian, 1932-
 Mystery at the mall.

 Summary: When coins are stolen from the coin shop in
the mall where her father is the manager, Jalinda tries
to find out who is responsible and the connection
between the missing coins and other items shoplifted
from other mall stores.
 [1. Mystery and detective stories] I. Stamm, Gwen,
ill. II. Title.
PZ7.H8112My 1985 [Fic] 85-13951
ISBN 0-8361-3401-X (pbk.)

MYSTERY AT THE MALL
Copyright © 1985 by Herald Press, Scottdale, Pa. 15683
 Published simultaneously in Canada by Herald Press,
 Kitchener, Ont. N2G 4M5. All rights reserved.
Library of Congress Catalog Card Number: 85-13951
International Standard Book Number: 0-8361-3401-X
Printed in the United States of America
Book design by Gwen Stamm

85 86 87 88 89 90 10 9 8 7 6 5 4 3 2 1

To my parents.

Acknowledgments

Thanks to Charlene Rule, who knows how malls operate, and to Goldie Hostetler, who knows children like Lyman, for reading this manuscript and giving suggestions.

Mystery at the Mall

1

I was sitting in my dad's office when I overheard Hal tell Marietta, "Old man Kline's really upset. He's missing a gold coin from his coin shop."

"What else is new?" she asked. "Things are being shoplifted every day."

"This coin's a rare one, though," he said. "It's worth $500."

None of us knew it then, but this missing coin was another clue that a mysterious thief was at work in Market Mall.

Before I go farther with this story, I'd better make some introductions. Hal is a security guard at Market Mall here in Travers City, Indiana. Marietta is the secretary of the mall manager, who is my dad, Karl Beam.

As for me, I'm a girl, eleven years old, average size with short brownish hair. I like school, but when school's out—weekends and summers— my hobby is "malling." That's what I call hanging around the mall. I usually come here after school, too. There's always something interesting to see or to do or to eat, or someone interesting to talk to.

One reason my dad lets me do this is because I don't have a mom at home—she died five years ago. He and I agree that malling is better than a sitter! And Dad, Lyman (my brother), and I often eat supper in one of the mall's restaurants or snackbars before going home after work in the evening.

Well, maybe you've noticed that I haven't told you my name yet. I've been trying to avoid it. But I guess I'll have to do it sometime, so it might as well be now. It's Jalinda Beam. Now that's not so bad, but no one calls me that. Unfortunately when I was five years old a neighbor boy, Brian Camp, had the idea my name sounded like "Jelly Bean." Everyone (but me) thought, "How cute!" And that's what I've been called ever since. Now that I'm a little older, my friends usually shorten it to "Jelly" or "Jell."

Can you guess then what Lyman's nickname is? "Lima Bean," of course, usually called "Lima" for short. My parents should have known better than to name him Lyman, but that was my mother's last name before she was married and they wanted to use it.

Lima's nine, but he doesn't do as much malling as I do. When he comes from his special school, he usually goes to Kiddy Kare in the mall. It's sort of like a day-care center for the kids of mall employees. Customers can leave toddlers there too while they're shopping, as long as the number of kids doesn't total more than 20. If it does, they have to take care of their own kids.

Like I said, Lima's nine, but he's more like a five-year old, and usually he likes to be with the little kids. When he doesn't, he follows me around, and then I'm responsible for him.

He has Down's syndrome. Dad says Lima will always be retarded and even when he's grown up, he'll be like an eight or nine year old kid. You don't need to feel too sorry for him, though! He's friendly and lovable (most of the time), and the clerks working in the mall stores always make a fuss over him and give him stuff. Sometimes it's enough to make me jealous. But other people who don't know him sometimes stare at him and make stupid remarks like, "Oh, what's wrong with that boy?" They seem to think he's deaf and can't hear what they're saying.

That's enough introductions for now. You'll get to know us better as the story goes on. Back to Mr. Kline's missing $500 coin. That sounded like something to liven up a dull June day, so I left the office and headed toward Kline's Koins to find out more.

It was 10:00 a.m. and the shops were just opening. Clerks were pulling aside or raising the fancy metal grills which closed off the stores from the halls (or concourses) during the night.

"Hi, Jelly," Fred called as he opened Fred's Fast Foods by clinking back the metal gate which had shut up his pizza and donut shop.

"Hi," I answered, going on by.

Then I spied an old white-haired man, cane in hand, walking briskly down the hall. He didn't look to the right or the left—no window-shopping for him. And he didn't seem to be waiting for a shop to open or to be heading for a certain store. What could he be doing? Was he possibly the coin thief trying to get away? Of course not. I was just trying to add a little excitement to the story. I knew very well who he was and what he was doing, clipping down the hall.

"Hi, Mr. Milton," I called, falling into step beside him. "How are you doing today?"

"Fine, young lady. I'm going to do two more laps, then sit by the fountain and rest a little. What're you up to today?"

Mr. Milton was one of our regular mall walkers who get their exercise here by doctors' orders. He'd had a heart attack and was supposed to walk every day. The mall was a perfect place for him to do it. The climate and temperature were always the same, no snow or rain or too much heat, and the distances were easy to count and measure.

I continued beside him. "What I'm up to is a visit to Mr. Kline. He's been robbed, so I'm going to check things out."

"Going to do some real-life detecting, eh?" he said. He knew how I liked to read mysteries and was always nosing around when anything unusual happened at the mall.

"Well, let me know if you need help with any clues you find," he went on. "Did I tell you I was a hotel detective before I was a hotel manager before I retired?"

"No, you didn't. Are you kidding me again, Mr. Milton?" I asked. With his twinkly gray eyes, it was hard to tell whether this was one of his tall stories or the truth.

"You don't think I look like a detective? Well, a detective isn't supposed to look like a detective, because if everyone can tell he's a detective, that hinders his detecting, you know," he said, not answering my question.

"Say, Mr. Milton, even if you weren't before, you'd have a good chance now. You could observe everything as you're walking, and no one would realize you're doing it!"

"Mmmm. Maybe," he said. "But remember, I don't want to get too excited after my heart attack. And I'm retired now. I'll let you do the work."

I was pretty sure he was kidding now. He was certainly not feeble because of his heart attack, and he didn't act like the kind of person who would retire by sitting somewhere in a corner on a rocking chair.

I didn't say anything more, though. After all, I didn't really want him to get involved. Because I wanted to do the detecting myself. I figured I was even less noticeable than he. Criminals wouldn't suspect a kid like me would be on their trail.

"Nope, I wouldn't want to interfere in your work," he went on. "Maybe you could regard me as a consultant if you need any help."

I didn't think I would, but you never know. "Thanks, Mr. Milton. I'll keep that in mind," I said.

By then we had arrived at Kline's Koins, so I turned off while Mr. Milton went on at his even pace.

There wasn't anyone else in the shop yet but Mr. Kline himself. This was my chance to investigate.

"Mr. Kline, I heard you were robbed. Where was the coin taken from?"

"Hello, Miss Beam," he said sadly, shaking his head. That was one thing I liked about him—he never called me Jelly.

"The gold coin was here," Mr. Kline said, pointing to an
empty spot on the velvet-covered shelf.

"Over here," he beckoned, and I followed him to a locked glass case. "It was locked like always this morning, but the coins were missing."

When he started to unlock it for me, I cried, "Oh, don't touch it!"

"You know all about this detective stuff, huh?" he said. "Well, don't worry. The police have been here already and checked for fingerprints."

I was disappointed, but then I don't know why I thought I would be the first one on the scene of the crime. After all, Hal had no doubt been here already too. Still, maybe I would see something the others hadn't noticed.

"The gold coin was here," he said, pointing to an empty spot on the velvet-covered shelf, "and the other coins were on each side of it."

"You mean more than one coin was stolen?"

"Oh yes, seven in all. But the others weren't so rare and valuable. So I'm not sure. Was it someone who knew coins very well and took that one on purpose and then took the others also to make me think they didn't know what they were doing?"

"Or was it someone who really didn't know what they were doing?" I finished.

"Did the police find any fingerprints?" I asked.

"Yes. They didn't tell me much about it. But I heard them say to each other that they looked like the fingerprints of a young person."

"How could anyone get in here, Mr. Kline? Didn't you have your gate closed?"

"I certainly did. And it was still closed and locked when I arrived here this morning. Can't figure it out."

Now that was mysterious. There was no other way into the shop. It was not like some of the other larger stores which had back entrances to the outside of the mall.

Before I could try to figure it out, I was distracted by someone pulling on my blouse.

"Hey, Jelly. Come and play. Daddy says you play with me."

It was Lima. What a time for him to show up and bother me—in the middle of an important case. Why didn't Dad consider what I wanted to do for once? But I had to admit that Dad didn't know about my wanting to be a detective. And I also had to admit that I didn't want him to know. If he did, he might not be too happy about my nosing around. So I figured that tending to Lima for a while would help to keep Dad in ignorance.

"Come on, then," I said. "Do you want to look at the fish and puppies in the Pet Parlor?" This was one of his favorite stores in the mall.

"No."

"Well, let's go to the library and find a Richard Scarry book." Our mall has a branch of the public library in it, and Lima loves the Scarry picture books.

"Yeah, liberry," he said.

Unfortunately, to get to the library from Kline's Koins, we had to go past La Belle Boutique. It sold very expensive women's clothes, but that's not why I didn't like to walk by it. It was because of Belle, the owner. Maybe if we walked by on the other side and pretended to look in The Jewel Box window, she wouldn't see us.

However, Lima apparently remembered the chocolate candy she'd lured him with the last time, and he pulled me right toward La Belle Boutique. Its windows were decorated this week with tiny pieces of cloth which turned out to be $75 swimsuits.

By then it was too late. Belle had seen us. "How's my sweet little Baby Lima today?" she gushed, patting his cheek. "And dear Jalinda, so kind to her brother. Your daddy must just be so proud of you. That reminds me, is he in the office today, dear? I do need to check with him about—about, uh—that crack in the ceiling." She pointed to an almost invisible line.

"Oh, don't bother," I said. "I'll tell him and he can send Sam, the maintenance man, over to look at it."

I knew it wouldn't do any good to say that. She'd think of some reason or other to talk to

Dad. She made me sick the way she was running after him. It kind of scared me, too. I didn't think he liked her, but I wasn't sure. She was striking-looking with her black upswept hair and her glamorous clothes. I used to be glad she'd ignore Lima and me, unless we happened to go by with Dad. Now she pounced on us even when he wasn't along.

"Candy," said Lima, holding out his hand.

"You're not supposed to eat any now!" I nearly hollered. I wished he wasn't so dumb as to play up to her.

Then his feelings were hurt. "Jelly not nice," he said.

"It won't hurt my little sweetie to have just one chocolate. Big sister will let you, Precious," she said.

"My *dad* doesn't want him to have candy between meals," I said. That ought to make her quit.

"Oh, well, then," she began to remove the candy. But Lima wasn't about to give up and he grabbed two chocolates.

"*Dad* sure won't like that," was my parting remark to her as I pulled Lima down the hall. When I glanced back, I saw she looked worried. Good, I thought. It's true that Lima is a little fat and Dad doesn't want him eating between meals, but I probably wouldn't mention it to him. I just wanted to give her a good scare.

When we were out of sight, I took one of the chocolates from him and ate it myself. He definitely shouldn't have two. And anyway, I like chocolates also.

Finally we got to the library and I found a Richard Scarry for him. I read to him a little, and then he got interested in the pictures, and I could slouch back in the orange beanbag chair and think about the missing coins, the newest theft.

I say newest theft because ever since summer vacation had started, at the beginning of the week, I had been trying to keep track of anything unusual at the mall. There was shoplifting going on every day, so that wasn't unusual. I wasn't especially interested in the shoplifters who were caught in the act, because there wasn't any case to solve there. What I was interested in was the things which were missing and that they didn't know what had happened to them. I would bug Hal and he usually didn't mind telling me about the things that had been reported to him as missing.

I took my little notebook out of my jeans pocket and looked over my list again. A transistor and cassettes from Music Master. Size 6 boys' shoes from ShoeShine. An apple pie from The Sweet Tooth. A small pizza and a dozen donuts from Fred's Fast Foods. A fur jacket from La Belle Boutique. A boys' shirt and shorts from Macho Man. Bread, sausage, and cheese from Friendly Farms. A suitcase from The Luggage Lair.

I looked again. I was hoping to see a pattern in what had been taken. It seemed unlikely, but what if one person was doing all the stealing and I could find out who! Transistor and cassettes, boys' shoes, apple pie, pizza and donuts, a fur jacket, boys' shirt and shorts, bread, sausage, cheese, and a suitcase. And now the coins. My thief must be a hungry boy who likes music and money, ready to travel in a lady's fur jacket! I almost laughed out loud in the library. Little did I know how close I was to discovering the secret I was looking for.

2

Lima was still looking at the pictures in his book, so I put my mind to trying to figure out how anyone could have gotten into Mr. Kline's shop. Someone small enough to squeeze through the grill? That didn't seem possible, but I should check to see exactly what kind of door closing he had. Maybe someone had sneaked Mr. Kline's keys and had duplicates made before returning them. I should find out where he keeps his keys. Or was it possible that someone had taken the coins before the store was locked last evening and Mr. Kline hadn't noticed? But how could they have removed the coins without breaking the glass on the case?

"Look, Jelly! See?" Lima interrupted my thoughts, talking out loud and pointing to a picture in his book. "Funny bear," he giggled.

I was embarrassed, sure that everyone was looking at us.

"Shhh," I said. Sometimes he thought that was a fun game and would say "Shhh" too. But other times he'd just keep talking loud. It didn't make any difference to him or embarrass him. This was one of those times.

"No shhh!" he called out and thumped the book down.

Time to leave, I thought and put the book back on the shelf.

"Come back again, Lima," said Brenda when we went by the book check-out desk.

"Bye, Brenna," he said loudly. The library ladies didn't seem to mind his loudness, but I didn't like it. Sometimes I longed for a nice, quiet, ordinary brother.

"Let's go see Mr. Kline," I said. I hoped I could get him to go there with me, though he wasn't much interested in the place. "He was robbed last night, Lima. Some of his coins were stolen. Maybe the police will be there."

I hardly thought they would be, but Lima was fascinated by policemen, and this might inspire him to come with me. I wasn't sure how much he understood of what I told him. Sometimes I would find out he had understood much more than I thought, while other times nothing seemed to sink in.

He went along willingly enough but instead of going with me into the shop when we got there, he started pulling me toward the fountain. There's a huge one in the center of the mall with steps going down to it and places to sit around it and some palms and other exotic plants to make it a restful spot.

"Coins in fountain," he said. "Come. Coins."

He hadn't understood. People often used the fountain like a wishing well, and he thought I was talking about the money people tossed there. Every so often Sam from maintenance cleans the fountain, and then all the coins are taken out and given for multiple sclerosis or something like that.

"No, coins in shop," I said, pulling him toward Kline's Koins. I was starting to talk like him!

"No, fountain. Come, Jelly."

I sighed. When he gets that stubborn, it's best to give in, or he might really raise a fuss. Maybe I could get him to come with me to Kline's Koins later. We walked down the carpeted steps to sit on the ledge around the fountain basin. It was relaxing to see the water swooshing upward and then to listen to it coolly splashing down.

"See," he pointed.

I looked down. Coins sparkled all over the bottom—quarters, nickels, dimes, pennies, their shapes wavering under the rippling water.

"See—pretty," he said. "Pretty, pretty."

When Mr. Kline saw his missing coin, he was ready
jump right in and get it.

Then I saw what he saw. My eyes widened in surprise. A coin not like the others! It was gold, with a strange design. I knelt down to get a better look, then jumped up.

"Lima, you're a better detective than I am. You wait here."

He grinned. I ran up the steps and to Mr. Kline's shop, calling to him to come quickly, to see if this was his missing coin.

When he saw it, he was ready to jump right in and get it. But I told him to wait and took off to the office to tell Dad. He had Sam turn off the fountain and get his long-handled rake before we came hurrying back. A crowd was gathering to see what was going on. Sam used his rake to scrape the coins to the edge of the fountain where he could reach in and get them.

Carefully he began lifting them out. Then there, glittering in his hand, was the $500 gold coin.

By then the big crowd surrounding us included Marietta and a newspaper reporter and photographer she had phoned to come (publicity helps mall business, you know). Cameras flashed as they took pictures of Mr. Kline beside Lima who was holding the coin and grinning like mad. I was glad for him. But I was jealous, too. After all, I was the one who was trying to be a detective.

But the mystery isn't solved yet, I reminded

myself. We didn't know who the thief was. And why would a person steal an expensive coin, then throw it away? And keep the ones which weren't valuable?

3

By the time the excitement had died down, Lima was ready to go to Kiddy Kare. And I could start again on my investigation.

Mr. Kline was back at his shop, busy directing a repairman who was installing a new lock in the case. While he was doing that, I sneaked a look at his grill. There was no way even a baby could squeeze through it.

So I asked him, "How could anyone get in here after you were closed, Mr. Kline?"

He just shook his head.

"Could the coins have been taken somehow before you closed last night? Or could someone have made duplicates of your keys and entered the shop and case that way?"

"I'll have to talk to Robert," he said. That's his

son who works some evenings for him. "He worked last night. I just came in to close up. I didn't look around that much. Just locked the cashbox and the door and we left."

"Hey, Kline," Fast Foods Fred came barging in. "How about this? Is this one of your missing coins?" He held up an old half dollar.

Mr. Kline looked it over. "Sure is," he said. "Where'd you get it?"

"Found it in my cash register just now. I asked the girls if they remembered getting it, and Louise thought she did."

"Who was it? Who gave it to her?" I asked eagerly.

"It was a boy, dark hair, about your size," he said to me. "He bought two donuts soon after opening time this morning. Louise didn't know about the robbery here, but she noticed it was an unusual coin and before she accepted it, she checked to be sure it wasn't some kind of foreign money. That's why she took note of who gave it to her."

Great! This was my chance. Fred wouldn't have told the police yet because he'd just now found out. I started down the mall, checking out every boy I saw. I could hardly believe how many dark-haired boys my size there were. I decided I'd better talk to Louise and find out more about the one who'd spent the half dollar. No luck. She didn't remember what he wore or if he'd been with someone else.

What could I do? I couldn't follow every dark-haired boy around. And besides, the one I wanted might be far away by now. Then I had another idea and hurried back to the coin shop.

"Mr. Kline, exactly what other coins were taken?"

"Why do you want to know? Why have you been asking so many questions, Miss Jelly?"

I could feel my face turning red. He must think I was really nosy. Calling me Jelly, too, when he knew I didn't like it. So I began to explain to him how I wanted to be a detective when I was old enough and how I wanted so much to get some practice now by solving a mystery.

"And why I want to know what the other coins are," I finished, "is so that I can check all the cash registers and see if any of them have been spent. And if any of them have been, maybe I can find out more about how the person looks who spent them."

"Good thinking, Miss Beam." I was relieved. He mustn't be mad—he didn't call me Jelly this time. "But do you know how many cash registers there are in this mall?"

I didn't, but I knew there were 50 stores, many with more than one register, and the three big department stores probably had at least ten each.

"That's the way detective work is, lots of hard, boring work," I said.

He told me then that the other five coins were also old fifty-cent pieces, similar to the one Fred had brought back.

What a job that turned out to be. I thought I knew nearly everyone who worked in the stores. I found out I didn't. Those who knew me didn't mind letting me look, though I could tell that some of them were just humoring the boss's silly daughter. Those who didn't know me, like the man in the Tux Shop or the fellow in Tom's Tobaccos looked at me like I was a nut, and kept a close eye on me when I inspected their cash drawers.

It was worth it, though. I did find two more of the coins. One turned up at Book World. Jackie, who's the manager, had noticed the coin and remembered an ordinary-looking boy spending it for a word puzzle book and a ballpoint pen. The other coin turned up at Dairy De-Lite. No one there had noticed it or could remember who had spent it. In both cases I put new coins in the registers to replace the old coins.

I took the old coins back to Mr. Kline and told him what I'd found out, which wasn't much.

All the time I kept looking for dark-haired boys my size (who weren't with their mothers), and all the time there were plenty of them around. By then it was 12:30 and I was hungry and tired of walking. I went back to Dairy De-Lite and bought a chocolate shake and a bag of chips. In the summer Dad usually lets me eat what I want at noon. Then at supper, when he eats with us, he makes sure I get enough vegetables and fruits.

I took the food and settled myself comfortably at one of the little tables at Dairy De-Lite. It felt good to sit down. I was halfway through my shake when I noticed one more dark-haired boy at a nearby table. Then my heart gave a big thump. He had finished a 50¢ Sundae Special and was sitting there writing in a word puzzle book with a ballpoint pen!

4

I gulped. What should I do now? Try to talk to him? Go look for Hal? Or bring Louise and Jackie here—they could identify him, if he was really the one.

I continued looking at him as I spooned up my shake. He didn't seem to be a tough guy or meanie type. So I wasn't scared of him, was I? I had to do something, but what?

He glanced up from his book and saw me staring at him. I looked quickly away. Well, one thing I could do was to see if the counter girl knew how long he'd been there. If he'd bought that sundae with the coin they'd had in the register, he must have been around quite awhile—even when I had come to check the register earlier.

I went to the counter. "Evie, how long has that boy been back there? The one in the corner with the book?"

She shrugged her shoulders. "I don't know."

"Oh, Jelly," said Frances, the other counter girl. "Here's another of those coins you were looking for."

I grabbed the half-dollar. "Who gave it to you? The boy back there?"

"Which boy? The little blond with his grandma?"

"No, no. The one with...." I looked back. He was gone! "He's not there. But he was dark-haired, my size, with a plaid shirt and navy shorts."

"I don't know. The coin came in during my break. Bill knew you were looking for old coins and he showed it to me when I came back ten minutes ago."

"Where's Bill? Maybe he'll remember."

"He's out for lunch," she said.

"I'll be back later," I called, rushing out. I looked both directions. The boy wasn't anywhere in sight. I turned to my right and sped down the hall, looking in every store as I went . But I knew that by the time I had checked out all 50 stores, he could be anywhere.

I slowed down as another idea hit me. For that, I needed to find Hal. I turned right at the fountain and went down the east-west concourse till I came to the office. He wasn't there, so I waited till Marietta finished typing the line she was on.

Before I could speak, she said, "I'm glad you came by, Jelly. Your father wants you to meet him at 5:30 at The Venice for supper."

"Okay," I said. "I'm looking for Hal. Do you know where he is?"

"He didn't mention going anywhere special, so I suppose he's just out making the rounds."

That meant more walking for me, but he was so tall that maybe it wouldn't take me too long to find him. Finally I did see him, looking at one of the cars. I guess I haven't mentioned that this was the week that all the car dealers had one or two of their new models on display down the centers of the concourses. People liked this because they could look over all the cars at once without having to go to the various dealers' showrooms. Dealers liked it, too. They had many more people looking at their cars than they would have had otherwise.

"You have one picked out?" I asked him.

"Nope. I'm keeping my old clunker," he said. "At least things this big (he patted the car) don't get shoplifted. But there are some nasty people around. Look at that."

He pointed to a scratch all along the side of the blue Datsun he'd been inspecting. Some people are hard to understand! Why would

Hal took his notebook from his hip pocket and flipped a
few pages. "Yeah, here it is," he said.

someone do that to a new car? However, that didn't have anything to do with what I wanted to know.

"Say, Hal, you know that boys' shirt and shorts that were stolen from Macho Man a few days ago? Do you have any more information about them, like what color they were?"

He took his notebook from his hip pocket and flipped a few pages. "Let's see.... Yeah, here it is. 'One blue and red plaid short-sleeved shirt, and one pair navy walking shorts.'"

"Bingo!" I said before I could stop myself.

"Now what does that mean?"

"And have you had any more reports today of stuff missing, since the coins were stolen?" I asked.

"No, I haven't. What're you on to, Jell? I'm supposed to be the law around here. You trying to take away my job?" he teased.

I wasn't ready to tell him my idea yet, not when I was so near to solving the mystery myself. I was sure I knew who the thief of the coins and the clothes was.

"Say, and what kind of shoes were those boys' shoes missing from ShoeShine?"

He checked. "Brown leather sandals."

I hadn't noticed what kind of shoes that boy had on, but I would sure look if I saw him again.

"Thanks, Hal."

I took off before he could question me any

more. I sat down on the first bench I came to, to take a look at the list in my notebook again. I checked off the shirt and shorts and put a question mark by the shoes. All the food on my list— apple pie, pizza, donuts, sausage, cheese, and bread could be things he stole to eat. The fur jacket and the suitcase and the transistor and cassettes—I couldn't figure out how they fit in. Maybe someone else had stolen those items. If this boy stole the rest, that would mean he had been around the mall for the last several days, stealing enough food to eat. Today he hadn't needed to steal any food because he had the stolen money to buy the donuts and the sundae.

It still didn't make sense though. He might steal food because he was hungry. But why would he steal clothes and then wear them right at the scene of the crime?

As for the gold coin, maybe he threw it away because he needed money he could spend in the mall, and he certainly couldn't have gotten away with spending that. Or maybe he thought the fountain would be a safe place to leave it until he could fish it out and pawn it.

A look at my watch showed me that it was soon time to meet Dad, so I went to the rest room to wash my hands and comb my hair.

The Venice is just about my favorite restaurant. Its walls are painted with canal scenes from Venice, and the waiters are dressed like gondoliers. (Gondoliers are the men who row gondolas. And gondolas are black wooden boats, shaped something like a canoe but with higher points on the ends. They're used to travel around in Venice which is a city in Italy built on islands. It has no streets, only canals, so you either have to travel by boat or walk. I'd love to go there some day.)

Anyway, let me tell you about the neatest part of this restaurant. When you enter, there's an actual canal going among the tables, and you step into a gondola to be rowed to your table. I don't get to eat there very often, because the prices make you think the food has been flown in special from Italy.

"Your father is already at his table," Alfredo, the head waiter, told me as he assisted me into the gondola. As romantic music played in the background, the gondolier, standing in the back of the boat, used his one long oar to row me through the dark. (The only light was from candles on the tables.) I guess Dad saw us coming because he was there to help me clamber out when we arrived at his table.

No one else was there, so I asked, "Where's Lima?"

"Just you and me," he said. "Lyman's been taken to supper by a friend."

I hardly knew what to say. I am practically never alone with my dad. Lima's almost always with us. Maybe Dad knew how I was feeling.

He said, "I don't get to talk to you very often, Linda. (That's the way he shortened Jalinda, and I liked it much better than Jelly.) You've been really good about doing your part with Lyman, even when you might not want to, and I appreciate it. So when Belle told me how she had all this extra food at her apartment and wanted to know if there wasn't some way she could help out, I thought she could entertain Lyman and we could be together once."

"What?" I burst out. Belle, of all people!

Dad just raised his eyebrows. "What do you mean, 'what'? Didn't I just explain?"

"Yes, but—" If he liked her, how could I come right out and say I couldn't stand her?

"Do I detect that you aren't too fond of Belle?"

"Yes. But I guess if you like her—"

"Give me credit for a little sense, Linda," he laughed. "After all, I could have sent you with her, or gone by myself, or we could have all gone."

"You mean—"

"Yes. I thought if she spent an hour or two with Lyman, it might help her decide to direct her overly friendly efforts somewhere else."

"Dad, you're mean!" I laughed.

"I hope not. I'm just trying to help Belle see life the way it really is."

We were interrupted by the waiter bringing

us the lasagne, tossed salad, and garlic bread which Dad had already ordered. As I began eating, I looked at him. To me he was nice-looking with his dark hair and moustache and glasses.

"Do you want a girlfriend, Dad?" I asked.

"I'd probably be ready to get married again, if I'd find the right person," he said. "We wouldn't be the easiest family to ask someone else to come into, though," he said.

"Jackie's nice," I said. Now what brought that popping out? I did think she was nice, the way she sometimes let me help her at Book World, but I had hardly been thinking of her as a possible next mother.

"Book World Jackie?" he asked.

"Yes."

"Interesting you'd say that. I think so, too. In fact we went out together a couple of times last month when you and Lyman were at Grandma Beam's. Now that I know you approve, maybe I'll try to see her some more."

"Well, enough about me and Lyman. How's the detective work going?"

My mouth dropped open. Luckily I didn't have any lasagne in it at the moment. "How did you know? That is, I mean, what detective work?"

"I can see it's time that we had a long talk. First you think I'd fall for Belle and her schemes. Then you think I don't know what my favorite daughter is doing?"

"I still don't know how you know."

"I'd think a good detective could figure it out! Let's see. At least five cashiers have told me things like 'Your daughter is so cute playing detective' or 'That daughter of yours is really going at it' or 'You should leave her at home, Beam.' And Hal has told me about your list. And Mr. Kline has informed me of some of your activities. And of course I've seen you in action here and there."

I felt awful. Tears were coming and I knew I wouldn't be able to stop them.

"Linda, honey, don't cry. I don't care that you're interested in something like this. It's good to help you develop logical thinking."

"I didn't want to do anything wrong," I wailed.

"I'm not saying you did anything wrong. But don't you think it would be better to check with me before you go digging into all the cash registers in the mall?"

I nodded.

"And you're not the police or Mall Security. You may come up with some helpful ideas, but if you do, share them. You're not a one-woman police and detective force. I don't want to scare you, but you could get yourself into trouble. We don't know what kind of person we're dealing with in these thefts."

"Yes, we do, Dad," I said. And I told him

everything I'd found out and suspected so far.

"You've done a good job and some good thinking, Linda," he said when I'd finished. "But can't you see that it would've been better to share this? If we'd had four or five people looking for this boy instead of only you, we'd probably have caught him by now."

"What about tomorrow, Dad?"

"Well, I'll fill Hal in on who we're looking for. You and I will keep our eyes open too. If we find him, we'll need to have Jackie and Louise take a look at him, and then see what happens from there. There's no way you can do that yourself. And I think you realized that when you saw him in the Dairy De-Lite, didn't you?"

"I guess so."

By then we'd finished our spumoni ice cream. Dad glanced at his watch. "It's a quarter till seven. We'd better get Lyman. I don't want to be too hard on Belle."

Instead of taking the boat, we walked back to the restaurant entrance.

"What about tonight?" I asked.

"There's nothing we can do for the moment. I suppose the kid will have gone home by now. And that's where we're heading too."

As we came from the restaurant into the corridor, way down at the end, I thought I saw that plaid shirt and blue shorts going into Deel's Department Store. Or was it just my imagination?

5

Belle was not her usual gushy self when we picked up Lyman. In fact, she looked a little tired. And I noticed when she told him good-bye, he was no longer her "Precious" but only "Dear." I smiled to myself. Dad's idea seemed to be working.

Because of my swimming class at the Y, I didn't get to the mall the next day until nearly 11:00. Dad wasn't in his office, so I didn't know whether he'd told Hal or what they were doing.

I went out to look around. Down the main drag I didn't see anyone—not Dad, nor Hal, nor the boy. I started going in and out of the shops. Still no one. Then I came to Deel's Department Store. I was going through the section where they sell TVs when I saw him.

There he was watching a news program. He was still dressed in his checkered shirt and blue shorts. "He looks so sad," I thought. I hadn't noticed that yesterday. Suddenly I wasn't scared of him. He seemed harmless. Besides, there were clerks and customers all around.

"Hi," I said. "What're you doing?"

He glanced at me. "Watching TV. What does it look like?"

"I saw you yesterday, too. I know most of the kids from around here, but I don't know you. Where're you from?" This wasn't strictly true— I did know lots of kids, but only those from my school.

"Bug off," he said.

Then I remembered. I still had one of the coins in my pocket—the second coin from the Dairy De-Lite that Frances had given me. I pulled it out. "Ever see any coins like this?" I asked, holding it in front of him.

He looked scared. "I don't know. Maybe. I'm not a coin collector."

"That's obvious, or you wouldn't have thrown away the one you did, would you? And we know you stole those clothes from Macho Man." I glanced at his feet, "And also those sandals from ShoeShine."

"Who're you anyway? You don't have any right to go around accusing people of stealing."

"My dad's the manager of this mall, that's

who, and being a detective is my hobby. I've found out all about you—where you spent the stolen coins yesterday and everything. And my dad knows too. We'll soon prove it when Louise from Fred's Fast Foods and Jackie from Book World see you. They'll remember you."

"Listen, maybe you're right, but don't tell. Please. If I can just hide out here another day or two, I'll be safe."

"What do you mean, safe?"

"Promise me you won't tell?"

"I can't. I've already told my dad what I've figured out, and he's going to be looking for you today. And so's Hal, the security guard."

"Then don't let them know you've seen me today. I'll—I'll find someplace to hide."

"But why hide? You haven't stolen all that much. You could soon pay back the stores. You might not even be arrested if you confess."

"It's not that. I've kept a list of everything I took, and my mom'll pay it all back. But I've got to hide till she gets here."

Nothing he said made much sense to me, and I said so.

"I'm hiding from my dad, stupid," he replied.

"I still don't get it."

"You've heard of parents kidnapping their kids, haven't you?"

"Not really. You mean that's what happened to you?"

"Yeah. Mom and Dad were divorced a couple of years ago. He was mean to her. Beat her up. Stuff like that. She got custody of me after the divorce and we moved from Michigan to California. She didn't want him to know where we were, because she didn't know what he might do.

"Somehow he found out where we were, because when I was coming out of school a week and a half ago, these guys in a car called me over to ask me for directions. They had me in the car and were driving off before I knew what was happening. There was my dad, in the backseat saying, 'Hi, Donny. Aren't you glad to see me? You'll be staying with me now.'

"I asked him about Mom. He said she didn't care if I went with him because she was having a hard time supporting us both. I didn't believe him. But I couldn't do anything about it. We started driving across the country. I kept looking for a chance to escape or to phone Mom, but he watched me every minute. When he stopped here four days ago, I got away. I hid under a bed upstairs in the furniture department of this store till everything closed up for the night."

"You mean you've been here ever since?"

"Yeah. I sleep on one of the beds up there and then roll under it when the clerks come in the morning to open up the store. Then I wait until I can safely sneak out. I stole these clothes because I thought it'd be harder for him to spot me if he comes back. He'll be looking for me to be wearing the same clothes I had on then."

"Does your mom know?"

"I called her collect the next day after I was here. She was frantic. Didn't know what had happened to me, and by then I'd been gone a week. She's going to fly here as soon as she can arrange it. So I've got to stay here till she arrives. Otherwise she won't know where I am."

"Donny, my dad'll help you. I know he will. Let me tell just him. He'll figure out some way to keep you safe till your mom comes."

I looked around to see if I could see Dad or Hal anyplace. Who should I see instead but my dear brother, heading our way and calling, "Jelly, Jelly."

"Oh, no," I groaned, "not now."

Donny must have looked up at the same time. I heard him mutter in a scared voice, "Dad!"

I stood up in front of him and whispered, "Go!"

"Well, hi, Lima," I called loudly, making a disturbance so Donny could get away.

I carelessly looked around to see if I could tell which person was Donny's dad. I almost shrank back. There wasn't much doubt which one it was. Why else would the black-haired man moving this way be giving me such a poisonous look?

6

Now I noticed Lima wasn't alone. Charlene, one of the Kiddy Kare aides, was with him.

"Oh, I'm glad we found you so soon, Jelly," she puffed. Charlene is overweight and keeping up with Lima had made her out of breath. "He wouldn't eat lunch with the other kids. Kept saying, 'Eat jelly. Eat jelly.' So I fixed him a jelly sandwich. He looked so disgusted and said, 'No! Eat Jelly sister!' "

Charlene laughed. "I finally figured out he meant he wanted to eat with you!"

"Okay, Charlene," I said. "I'll take him for lunch." This would give me a chance to get away from Donny's beady-eyed father who was listening to every word. Donny had disappeared by then. Probably by now he was under one of the beds upstairs.

"Come on, Lima. Let's go get some of Fred's pizza. You like that."

"Yes. Like pizza. Like Jelly too. No eat Jelly last night. Eat Jelly now."

After we'd left Deel's and were going down the hall, I looked back and saw Donny's dad following us. I didn't much care for that. Still, there was one advantage. It would take him away from where Donny was.

That pizza smell would have guided us to Fred's even if we hadn't almost known the way with our eyes shut. I bought us each two slices of pepperoni pizza, and a carton of milk to start with. Yes, I know Pepsi goes with pizza, but I don't often drink pop—it's not good for you.

Where we were sitting at the counter I could look out into the mall. Across the way was a newsstand, and there was Donny's dad, supposedly looking at some paperbacks and magazines. I knew he was really keeping a watch on us. At least that way he wasn't searching for Donny.

We each had a slice of sausage pizza and a second carton of milk to finish up on. I was just about to say, "Now Lima, are you ready to go back to Charlene?" when I decided not to. As long as he was with me, Beady-eyes was keeping his distance.

"Let's go find Dad, Lima," I said instead. I really needed to see him. I hadn't promised Donny I wouldn't. And anyhow, he'd asked me not to tell before we knew his dad was around. Maybe now he'd *want* me to tell him.

Lima came along willingly. It wasn't far to Dad's office. I didn't even look back this time. I didn't care if the man followed me there or not."

Dad still wasn't in! "Marietta, where's Dad?" I asked. "I have to see him."

"He was in only a minute or two this morning, just long enough to tell me he'd be gone till midafternoon. He's meeting with some people who're interested in those spaces we have to rent, you know, where India Imports and the Card Corner used to be."

"Do you know if he talked to Hal at all while he was here?"

"Definitely not. Because Hal called in sick this morning, so he hasn't been here at all."

Oh boy. What should I do? "Did Dad say anything about supper?"

"No. I suppose he's planning to eat with you two as usual."

"Thanks, Marietta. Just tell him when he comes in that I need to see him right away. I'll be—tell him I'll be somewhere near the J. C. Penney store." That was at the opposite end of the mall from Deel's. If that guy still wanted to follow me, we would be far away from where I

The man grabbed my arm. "I want to talk to you about my son," he said.

thought Donny probably was.

I took Lima back to Kiddy Kare and deposited him with Charlene. I had decided I would go to Book World. Sometimes Jackie let me help unpack books and prepare them for the shelves. Also Book World wasn't far from Penneys, and later on I could begin to keep a lookout for Dad.

I didn't make it to Book World though. "Jelly," someone called softly behind me. I turned around. There the man was, right behind me, smiling in a way I didn't trust.

How did he know my name? He must have heard Lima call me that.

The man grabbed my arm. "I want to talk to you about my son. I saw you talking to him this morning."

"I don't know you. How would I know your son?"

"Back there in Deel's you were talking to him. Don't deny it."

"I was talking to my *brother* in Deel's."

"You mean that retard? Not him. The boy you were talking to before."

That made me mad. "My brother may be mentally retarded. But I know some people who just *act* that way!" I stared right at him.

Then he gave me that oily smile again. "Sorry. It's just that I'm worried about my boy. And I know you were talking to him."

"Why're you worried about him?"

"I need to keep a watch on him. He's, well, when he gets in a mall he's likely to do a lot of stealing. He's practically a kleptomaniac. I don't want him getting in trouble."

"Then why don't you take him home instead of following me all over the place?"

"That's exactly what I want to do, take him home, as soon as you tell me where he is."

"You'll have to find him yourself, I guess, or wait till he comes home tonight. Because I don't know where Donny is."

"How'd you know his name if you don't know him?"

Oh no, I'd made a slip. "I suppose he told me."

"What else did he tell you? Look, I'm sorry to say this about my own kid, but he lies a lot too. I'll bet he told you some stories about me. That's why you won't tell me anything. Did he pull that one on you about my kidnapping him?"

I must have looked startled, because he went on, "That's Donny. He tried that one before when he got in trouble. His mother and I just don't know what to do with him anymore. And he looks so innocent when he does it. I'm not surprised you believed him."

My mind was racing. I had completely believed Donny. Now I wasn't sure. Could his father be telling the truth? Maybe it was just the idea about his father that had formed in my mind when Donny was talking about him which had made this man look so dangerous to me. I looked at him again. He was waiting, a kindly expression on his face.

"Come on, I just want to help Donny. The sooner we get him back home, the better it'll be for him."

"Do you and your wife live around here?" I asked.

"Why, yes. We haven't been in the community too long, but we live in Kingston Apartments," he said.

There *was* a group of apartments nearby with that name. But that didn't mean he lived there. He might have driven past them. I didn't know what to think. I thought of telling him he would have to talk to my dad. But he was so convincing. I wanted Dad to hear Donny's side too.

I finally said, "I don't know where he is. As you saw, after my brother came, he was gone. Would you like to talk to the mall security guard?" I knew Hal wasn't here so he couldn't talk to him, but I wanted to see how he would react to the suggestion.

"No, no. I don't want the boy to get in trouble."

So I still didn't know. Was it really Donny or himself that he didn't want to get in trouble?

"What would you know about the mall security guard anyhow?" he went on.

"Oh, he's a friend of mine. And my dad's the

mall manager, too." I might as well get him worried, in case he really was the bad guy Donny had said he was.

"Sure," he said, "and I'm Santa Claus." His hand tightened on my arm.

"Jelly, is anything wrong?" a voice behind me asked. I turned to see Jackie standing there.

"I was just asking the little lady for directions," the man said and walked quickly away.

"Who in the world was that?" she asked.

"I don't know," I answered. It was the truth. I didn't know his name. "I was on my way to see if you needed any help with unpacking books."

"Sure. Come along."

I was quiet as we walked together, trying to think what to do. I'll wait a little and tell Dad the whole thing, I decided. I hoped he'd show up soon!

7

Usually I loved to look over the books that were coming in, especially if there were any mysteries for kids. Since I was working for free, when I unpacked books I could take time to read about the stories on the backs of the books or on the inside of the covers. I could read parts of any I thought might be interesting. Today I didn't bother. I was too edgy. Before putting them on the shelves, I had to place little price stickers in the hardback books. Most of the paperbacks already had their prices printed on them.

After I worked awhile back in the children's department, I asked Jackie if there was something I could do nearer the entrance. I needed to keep a lookout for Dad. She had me unpack some books for the romance section near the door. Work there went faster because I had no interest in books like *Raging Torrent of Love* or *Delirious Desire* with their pictures of loving couples on the covers.

By 5:15 still no Dad, so I told Jackie good-bye and took a quick walk by Penneys. Then I headed toward the office. When I was passing La Belle Boutique, Belle spotted me and beckoned me to come over. What now? I went reluctantly.

Who should be standing behind her but Donny's dad. At least it wasn't *my* dad with her!

"This gentleman has told me about his son," she said, "and really, dear, you should tell him where the boy is. That fur jacket he took from me is worth $2,000."

"I've told him I don't know where his son is. But why do you think the boy would steal a woman's fur jacket?"

"Oh, he doesn't know the worth of things," said his father. "Probably just thought it would be something pretty for his mother."

"That jacket's been missing a couple of days. You mean he brought it home to your apartment?" I asked.

"I haven't seen it—he probably hid it—but I'll certainly check when I get home."

If you have an apartment. If you go home, I thought. *And why don't you go and check right away instead of accusing your own child with no evidence?* I wondered, too, why Belle was talking so freely with a stranger. I supposed the reason was that he was good-looking in a smooth, dark-haired way.

"Maybe we should talk to Karl about it," Belle said to him. "I mean Karl Beam, our mall manager, and *her* father," she said motioning toward me. *She wants to show off her new friend to my dad,* I thought. *Well, Dad won't be jealous.*

"I'm on my way there now," I said. "But I don't think he's in, so don't bother." I certainly didn't want them around when I finally had a chance to bring Dad up to date.

I decided he didn't want to see Dad. He didn't encourage her to go, or offer to go with her. So she didn't come either. She certainly wasn't going to go anywhere if this good-looking man didn't go with her.

I said, "So long, Belle. So long, Santa Claus."

"Now, why did she call you that, Mr. Colton?" I heard her say in her flirty voice as I went on. So now I knew Donny's last name—at least if his father had given his real name to Belle.

At the office Marietta handed me a note. "Your father phoned in and gave me this message for you," she said. The note read, "Tell Linda I'm sorry I couldn't be there today. We'll talk tonight. She should get Lyman and a carryout dinner for us from Yang Lin's and go home. I'll try to be there by 6:30."

I thought of Donny. Was he still hiding, not sure of where his father was? If he *wasn't* around, that would mean he had some place to go, and his story that he had to wait till his mother came wasn't true. If he *was* still here, then his story was true, and he'd be awfully hungry, not having dared to come out to get food.

I decided that if Mr. Colson wasn't in sight when I went for Lima and the food, I'd go quickly to Deel's second floor and look for Donny. However, there Mr. Colton was by the fountain where he could keep an eye on the traffic from all directions. He hadn't given up.

I couldn't chance the trip to Deel's, so I went on to Yang Lin's and put in an order for egg rolls, sweet and sour pork, and egg fu yung. Then I went to get Lima from Kiddy Kare, and came back to pick up the food. We walked out, across the parking lot, and down the sidewalk two blocks to our house. I took the mail from our box and picked up the newspaper from the porch before unlocking the door.

Lima wanted to eat right away, but I told him we would wait for Dad. I found *Sesame Street* for him on TV, and he watched that while I put the food on three plates and slipped them into the microwave oven. It would only take a minute to heat the food after Dad came. Then I cut some lettuce and put it on three salad plates. I carried them to the table along with a bottle of Thousand Island dressing and a bottle of soy sauce.

Then I found the library book I had begun reading the day before. It was an exciting story called *Caught in a Cave,* but I couldn't concentrate on it. There was too much real life excitement to think about.

8

It was 6:29 when I finally heard Dad at the door. "Hi, kids," he called from the hall.

When he came into the living room he said, "You didn't have the door locked, Linda. You know I always want you to keep it locked, especially when you're home alone."

"I forgot this time, Dad, with the food and the mail and the paper to carry in. And I have so much to tell you, too. My mind was on that."

He had flicked the oven on and our food was ready almost before I had finished talking.

We sat down at the table and Lima said a prayer. He said his favorite which is, "God is great and God is good, and we thank him for our food. By his hand we all are fed. Give us, Lord, our daily bread."

After Lima finished, he looked at us proudly. He hadn't forgotten any part of it this time! I hugged him and said, "That was very good, Lima." All the hours I had spent helping him learn it were worth it.

"So, it sounds like you found out something else today," Dad said as we began eating.

"I found out too much," I said, "so much that I don't know what's true!" I told him everything Donny had said, then everything Mr. Colton had said. "So Dad, who would *you* believe?"

"Bad boy! Bad man!" Lima said. We both looked at him in surprise. He had been listening, but I hadn't expected him to understand that much.

"I wonder if you're asking a question—are they bad—or making a statement—they are bad," Dad said. "As for me, I need to know more before deciding. I think what I'd like to do is go over to the mall after closing time, 9:30 or 10:00. The father may have gone to his apartment or motel or whatever by then. I'd like to see whether the boy is around somewhere, and talk to him. Like you said, if he *is* around, that'll be a sign in his favor. I'll have to check with Paul Stanton first. His cleaning crew does most of the stores in that end of the mall, including Deel's. If they're going to be around about that time, they can let me into Deel's. If not, maybe Paul will let me use his key."

Dad did some phoning and then came back to say that Paul's people were working an early morning shift but that he would let Dad use the Deel's key.

"Did you tell him why you wanted it?" I asked.

"Not exactly. Just that I wanted to check on something regarding some recent thefts."

"Dad, I can go too, can't I?" I begged. "Please! Donny knows me and won't be so scared if I'm there. And it's sort of my case, after all. Please, Dad!"

"There's no need to whine around like that," he said sternly, then smiled, "because I was planning to take you along anyway!"

Sometimes I wish I'd catch on quicker when he's teasing.

"Put that stuff in the dishwasher, Linda," he said, "and I'll go next door and see if Mrs. Hilliard can stay with Lyman while we're gone."

We watched the news on TV, then I tried again to read my book while Dad read the paper. Next we played a couple games of "Uno." It's a game Lima can play, too, with a little help once in awhile. After that Dad had me get Lima ready for bed while he went to Stanton's for the key. At 9:45 Mrs. Hilliard came.

Our house is a duplex and she lives on the other side. She's a widow, about 60 years old and very nice. For example, when her grand-children come to visit and she bakes cookies, she always gives us some, too.

"Thanks for coming, Mrs. Hilliard," Dad said. "We shouldn't be gone more than half an hour, or an hour at the most."

The mall looked so different at night. Some of the huge parking lot lights were still on, but the lots themselves were empty and quiet. The rows of white cement parking guards made me think of tombstones lined up in a cemetery.

Dad got out his keys and unlocked the en-trance near his office, locking it again behind him as we went in.

The hall was only dimly lit. The stores on each side were dark and dead. My sneakers didn't make any sound, but Dad's footsteps echoed in the stillness. It was creepy. Not even a friendly splash from the fountain—it was shut down for the night.

At Deel's, Dad unlocked the grill and pushed it back just far enough for us to go through. We came to the clothes department first. The dark-ness had changed their bright colors to black and gray, so now they looked like they were waiting there in the gloom for someone to wear them to a funeral.

In the TV department where I'd found Donny that morning, the screens were blank and life-less. Even the escalator had died. We walked up

Donny wasn't under any of the beds, although I did find his puzzle book and pen.

its unmoving steps, the only time I've ever gone up the down side.

Upstairs our feet were noiseless on the carpet as we walked by the displays of china and housewares, past the towels and bedding to the furniture department.

As we neared the beds, Dad nodded to me. I called softly, "Donny, Donny," but my voice seemed to boom out. "It's me, Jelly. Are you here?"

There was no answer. Dad went over to the display of lamps and light fixtures and began turning some of them on.

"Donny," I called again. "It's safe for you to come out."

There was enough light to see now, and also enough that he couldn't sneak out from under a bed to go hide somewhere else. I began to lift up the spreads and look under the beds. There were only six, and he wasn't under any of them, although I did find his puzzle book and pen.

I was so disappointed. I guess I had really counted on him being there.

"Just a minute," Dad said. "I have an idea." He walked over to the rest rooms by the store restaurant, The Upper Room, and went into the men's room.

When I got near I heard a scuffling sound and a cry of "No!" so I pushed the door open and peered in.

"Donny, it's okay," I called. "It's my dad, and we want to help you."

I don't know if he believed me or if he just gave up, but he let Dad lead him out of the rest room and over to the couches where Dad sat him down on one.

Dad said, "Linda's told me—"

"Who's Linda?" he interrupted.

"Jelly, then. Her name's actually Jalinda, and I prefer Linda to the Jelly most people call her. So does she. Anyway, Jelly's explained to me what you told her this morning."

Donny's scared expression changed to a more hopeful one.

"What you don't know," Dad went on, "is that your father talked to her later," and he informed Donny what his father had said to me.

"He's lying! That's not true!" Donny burst out.

"You can see why we don't know for sure, can't you, Donny?" Dad said. "But there's an easy way to find out the truth. You give me your mother's name and address and phone number, and I'll call her to find out."

I held my breath. Would he have it to give, or would he have to admit he had been lying?

"Sure, I'll give them to you. It's Ms. Donna Colton, 2644 West Shore, Santa Monica, 213-448-3621. But what if she's already left?"

I began breathing again and smiled.

"Don't worry," Dad said. "I'll call directory assistance and ask for her number at that address. And if that checks out, I'll know you're telling the truth. And then I'll also call her and let her know you're okay—if she isn't already on her way."

Donny's face changed completely. It was the first time I saw him smile.

"Turn out the lights, Linda," Dad said, "and we'll go down to the office and call."

This time we down the up escalator. It was as dark as ever below, but the store was no longer deathlike in its stillness—it was only peacefully sleeping, resting so it would be ready for the busy day ahead.

The call to directory assistance showed Donny had told the truth, but Dad couldn't reach his mother. She was either out somewhere or on her way here.

"You'll come and spend the night with us—no more sleeping on or under Deel's bed," Dad said, locking up.

"I'll bet you haven't eaten since breakfast, Donny," I said as we were cutting across the parking lot and heading toward home. "Were you hiding all day?"

"Yeah," he said. "I was under the bed the whole time, till I heard noises on the escalator steps. There was no light, so I knew it wasn't the cleaning people who sometimes come to work at night. I got scared then. I'm not sure why I thought the rest room would be safer. I'm glad you looked there."

"Something's got to be done about that man, Dad," I said. "He can't just go around kidnapping people, can he?"

"I'm not sure what our laws on that are so far as parents are concerned. I'll find out in the morning. I think now all we'll worry about is a good night's sleep for this fellow—after some food."

Mrs. Hilliard left as soon as we arrived, and we went on to the kitchen where I fixed Donny two hot dogs and some lettuce salad. Dad got out ice cream for everyone—including Lima, who had waked up and come to the kitchen dressed in his pajamas.

"Bad boy?" he said pointing to Donny.

"No, good boy. Bad man," I said.

9

When I awoke the next morning, it was 8:30. From the kitchen I could hear Donny's and Lima's voices, so I quickly dressed and went to join them. They were both eating cornflakes, and I poured myself a bowlful too.

The first thing I saw when I sat down at the table was a note from Dad. "Kids—Come to the mall at 10:00. Be sure to *come to my office first.* If I'm not there, *wait* there until I come."

"Why do you think he wrote that?" Donny asked.

"I suppose he doesn't want you to go where your dad'll see you until he's talked to us first," I answered. "I wonder what he's found out."

"You said you were keeping a list of what you

stole so your mom could pay back the stores," I went on. "I'm practicing to be a detective, so I'll give you *my* list of what I think you took, and you see if I'm right, okay?"

"Okay," he said.

"Boys' leather sandals from ShoeShine," I read. "A plaid shirt and navy shorts from Macho Man. An apple pie from The Sweet Tooth. A pizza and a dozen donuts from Fred's Fast Foods. Bread, sausage, and cheese from Friendly Farms, and seven coins from Kline's Koins. Now did I miss anything?"

Donny sat there wide-eyed. "No, that's everything. I knew you'd figured out some of it, but how'd you know all that?"

So I explained how my great detective brain had worked things out. But it hadn't discovered everything, so I asked, "How did you get the coins from Mr. Kline's shop and why did you take them?"

"I had to steal food so often that I was scared I'd get caught. So I thought if I could steal some money, I'd only have to do that once and then I'd have it to spend. I was hanging around the coin shop at near closing time. There were other people in the store besides me. The clerk unlocked one case with a little key and showed some coins to two of them. They didn't want the coins, so he locked the case again and went on to show them something else, but he left the key lying on the case. While he was busy with them, I took the key, unlocked the case, grabbed the first coins I could find and locked the case again. I put the key down and the coins in my pocket and left. I had to hurry back to Deel's before they closed up, and I didn't hear anyone calling after me, so I suppose he didn't notice what I'd done or that anything was missing.

"Then when I had time to look the coins over, I knew I couldn't spend that gold one, so the next morning I tossed it in the fountain. When I saw all those coins in there already, I thought that if I needed more money before Mom got here, I would try to figure out some way to get some of them out of the water."

"You know that coin you threw away was worth $500?"

"Honest? So that's what all the fuss was about! I saw that guy fish it out and people taking pictures and everything."

We placed our breakfast dishes in the dishwasher to join those from yesterday. I thought it looked about full enough, so I dumped in some soap powder and turned the washer on.

While Lima was watching *Captain Kangaroo reruns*, Donny asked me, "What's wrong with your brother? I never saw anyone like him."

I told him how Down's syndrome is something you're born with and that doctors know it's caused by an extra chromosome but don't know what causes that extra chromosome. "People used to call kids who have it 'mongoloids' because of the way their eyes are," I explained. "Did you notice his eyes have a sort of Chinese-y look? Also Down's syndrome kids often have tongues too big for their mouths. That's one reason they can't talk very well."

"He won't get better, will he?"

"No, he'll always be like a little kid."

"Well, he's a nice kid. Your dad's nice too. Do you always stay with him instead of your mom? Where does she live?"

"Yeah, we're always with Dad. My mom was killed in a car accident five years ago." I didn't like to talk about it.

"Sorry," he said. "I should know that just because there isn't both a mom and dad in a family doesn't mean there's been a divorce."

"Woops, look at the time," I said. "We should get going."

When we arrived at the office Dad was there, and also Hal and another man. I noticed that Hal wasn't wearing his uniform and soon found out why. Dad ushered us all into his private office except for Lima. Marietta got the job of entertaining him.

Dad introduced everyone. The man I hadn't known was Detective Lieutenant Harris. A real police detective!

Lt. Harris took charge. He said, "Mr. Beam has told us the whole situation. We've already checked with the police in Santa Monica. Your mother," he said to Donny, "had reported you missing and told the police she suspected your father was behind it. She later told them about your phone call and that she was leaving yesterday to fly here.

"Now what we want to do is to pick up your father, if he's still around. I think he will be," Lt. Harris said. "He knows this is where you escaped from him, and yesterday he saw you were still here, so I figure he'll be back today for another look.

"What we want you to do is to walk around the mall," Lt. Harris continued, "but stay mainly in the fountain area. Hal will be where he can watch you. We hope that way your father will try to take you again. We'll have a much stronger case against him if we can catch him in the act."

It sounded pretty exciting! But I wouldn't have any part in it. It was "my" case and I'd probably have to watch the evening news to see how it came out.

Then I realized Lt. Harris was talking to me. "What?" I said.

"I understand you met Mr. Colton yesterday. Would you recognize him again?"

"Oh, yes!"

"Okay. I'd like you to walk around too—not with Donny but not too far away. I'll be nearby. Signal me if you see Mr. Colton. Then I'll be able to keep him under observation until he makes his move. Will you do that?"

"I'd love to!" I said. I was going to be working as an undercover policewoman!

"You take Lyman with you," Dad said.

"Oh, Dad. You know how he is. He'll want to go just where he wants to. Why can't he stay at Kiddy Kare?"

"You'll look less suspicious if Lyman is with you," Dad said.

"Good idea, Mr. Beam," said Lt. Harris. I was outnumbered.

I soon learned that undercover work can be boring. We strolled here and strolled there, looking in windows or talking to clerks we knew while I still kept an eye open for Mr. Colton. No Mr. Colton anywhere. One endless hour went by. At least Lima was being cooperative.

Then I saw Mr. Milton on his daily walk and thought we would join him for a while. I could do that and still watch.

"Hello, Miss Beam and Mr. Beam," he said as we fell in step. "Have you solved any cases yet?"

"Yes, I have. But there's still a little work to finish on it. In fact, right now," I lowered my voice, "I'm working for the police. We're after a criminal who—I'd better not tell you any more.

It's confidential, you know."

He nodded his head. Lima couldn't keep up with Mr. Milton, so we dropped behind. I gazed at the fabrics in the Sew So Nice windows, trying to look interested. Then I looked around to see if I could spot Lt. Harris. He was behind us eating a doughnut from Fred's.

That made me hungry so I bought Lima and me each a blueberry doughnut, and we went to sit by the fountain to eat them. I waved at Mr. Milton who was taking his rest period nearby. I noticed Donny was standing by the J. L. Terry Variety Store, looking at the swimming and picnic equipment in their window.

I took a couple of more bites of my doughnut. When I glanced up again, Donny was closer, in front of Kline's Koins. As I was watching, two men grabbed his arms and started to pull him away. I didn't recognize either of them. What should I do? And where was Hal? I couldn't see him anywhere. Lt. Harris had seen the commotion too. He came to the bench where I was sitting and looked at me questioningly. I shook my head no. He started walking in the direction of Donny and the men anyway.

Then I saw a figure quietly appear from where it had been hiding among the palm trees. Mr. Colton! I couldn't signal to Lt. Harris when his back was turned toward me, so I called out, "It's him! Here he is!" Mr. Colton started to run

*I saw a figure quietly appear from among the palm trees.
"It's him! Here he is!" I shouted.*

swiftly up the steps around the fountain.

Lima jumped up and shouted, "Bad man! Bad man going!"

Lt. Harris turned toward us, but he was too far away. Mr. Colton would escape!

But instead of escaping, he was suddenly lying flat on his stomach on the floor, the breath knocked out of him. Mr. Milton had neatly caught Donny's father's leg with the curved end of his cane and tripped him.

Lt. Harris was there asking, "Is this the one?"

"Yes," I said.

He snapped handcuffs on him and started marching him toward the office. I looked back to where Donny and the two men had been struggling. Now there were four men. My father and Hal had hold of the two strangers and were forcing them toward the office. Donny was following, grinning.

"Lima," I said, "you did a good job in helping catch the bad man. And Mr. Milton, you're a hero."

"Was this the criminal you were after in your confidential work?" he asked.

"Yes, but I'll have to tell you about it later," I said. "I want to find out exactly what was happening. Come on, Lima. Let's see the policeman at the office." He wouldn't know about plainclothes policemen, but maybe Lt. Harris would have a badge he could show him.

"Donny, wait," I called trotting after him. "Who were those two guys?"

"I saw them once before. They're friends of my dad's, I guess. They're the two who pulled me into their car by my school. I think he must have had them come here to help him again."

As we walked down the hall I noticed this pretty lady standing in front of The China Cupboard. She was staring at Donny. I poked him. "Look down there."

"Mom!" he yelled and ran to hug her.

* * *

I don't think I need to tell you everything that took place in the office to wind the case up or what happened in court later. I will just inform you that the bad guys were eventually punished, and the good guys (Donny and his mom) went to California to live happily ever after (I suppose).

So my first case was completed. I deserved a vacation. But—in this job there's never time off. There was still work to do. Who had taken that fur jacket anyway? And the transistor and the suitcase?

The Author

Marian Hostetler is a third-grade teacher in the Concord Community Schools, Elkhart, Indiana, who has had experience as well in overseas settings—Algeria, Chad, and Nepal. She is also interested in archaeology and has participated in digs in Cyprus and Tunisia. During the 1985-86 school year she is taking a sabbatical leave from teaching and is working for the Mennonite Board of Missions, based in Elkhart, in the French-speaking countries of Ivory Coast and Benin in West Africa.

Concerning this book, she says, "A part of every American child's life is 'going to the mall,' so a mall seemed to me to be a good setting for a story, one with which we can all identify. A mall is really a city in miniature. Under one roof is everything a person could need or want (except perhaps places to sleep and to worship). It is a place for browsing and looking and buying and meeting friends."

Her other books published by Herald Press are *African Adventure, Journey to Jerusalem, Fear in Algeria,* and *Secret in the City.* She has also written 13 short missionary biographies which are available for churches to use in children's classes in a booklet called *God's Messengers.*

Marian is originally from Orrville, Ohio, and is an active participant in the life of Belmont Mennonite Church in Elkhart.